'SUMMER
WAS DRAWING
TO A CLOSE,
AND I REALIZED
THAT THE
BOOK WAS
MONSTROUS.'

JORGE LUIS BORGES
Born 1899, Buenos Aires, Argentina
Died 1986, Geneva, Switzerland

'The Garden of Forking Paths' was first published in 1941 in
El jardín de senderos que se bifurcan (1941), and subsequently in
Ficciones (1944). 'The Book of Sand' was first published in 1975
in *El libro de arena*. 'The Circular Ruins' was first published in
1941 in the literary journal *Sur*, and subsequently in *El jardín
de senderos que se bifurcan* (1941) and *Ficciones* (1944). 'On
Exactitude in Science' was first published in the March 1946
edition of *Los Anales de Buenos Aires, año 1, no. 3*. 'Death and
the Compass' was first published in 1942 in the literary journal
Sur, and subsequently in *Ficciones* (1944).

BORGES IN PENGUIN MODERN CLASSICS
The Aleph
The Book of Sand and Shakespeare's Memory
Brodie's Report
Fictions
Labyrinths
Selected Poems
The Total Library
A Universal History of Iniquity

JORGE LUIS BORGES

The Garden of Forking Paths

Translated by
Donald A. Yates, Andrew Hurley
and James E. Irby

PENGUIN BOOKS

PENGUIN CLASSICS

UK | USA | Canada | Ireland | Australia
India | New Zealand | South Africa

Penguin Books is part of the Penguin Random House group
of companies whose addresses can be found at
global.penguinrandomhouse.com.

Penguin
Random House
UK

This selection first published 2018
003

Set in 11.2/13.75 pt Dante MT Std
Typeset by Jouve (UK), Milton Keynes
Printed and bound in Great Britain by Clays Ltd, Elcograf S.p.A.

ISBN: 978–0–241–33905–3

www.greenpenguin.co.uk

Contents

The Garden of Forking Paths

On page 252 of Liddell Hart's *History of World War I* you will read that an attack against the Serre-Montauban line by thirteen British divisions (supported by 1,400 artillery pieces), planned for 24 July 1916, had to be postponed until the morning of the 29th. The torrential rains, Captain Liddell Hart comments, caused this delay, an insignificant one, to be sure.

The following statement, dictated, reread and signed by Dr Yu Tsun, former professor of English at the *Hochschule* at Tsingtao, throws an unsuspected light over the whole affair. The first two pages of the document are missing.

'. . . and I hung up the receiver. Immediately afterwards, I recognized the voice that had answered in German. It was that of Captain Richard Madden. Madden's presence in Viktor Runeberg's apartment meant the end of our anxieties and – but this seemed, *or should have seemed*, very secondary to me – also the end of our lives. It meant that Runeberg had been arrested or murdered.[1] Before the sun set on that day, I would encounter the same fate. Madden was implacable. Or rather, he was obliged to be so. An Irishman at the service of England, a man accused of laxity and perhaps of treason, how could he fail to seize and be thankful for such a miraculous opportunity: the discovery, capture, maybe even the death of two agents of the German Empire? I went up to my room: absurdly I locked the door and threw myself on my back on the narrow iron cot. Through the window I saw the familiar roofs and the cloud-shaded six o'clock sun. It seemed incredible to me that that day without premonitions or symbols should be the one of my inexorable death. In spite of my dead father, in spite of having been a child in a symmetrical garden of Hai Feng, was I – now – going to die? Then I reflected that everything happens to a man precisely, precisely now. Centuries of centuries and only in the present do things happen; countless men in the air, on the face of the earth and the sea, and all that really is happening is happening to me . . . The almost

1. An hypothesis both hateful and odd. The Prussian spy Hans Rabener, alias Viktor Runeberg, attacked with drawn automatic the bearer of the warrant for his arrest, Captain Richard Madden. The latter, in self-defence, inflicted the wound which brought about Runeberg's death. (Editor's note.)

intolerable recollection of Madden's horselike face banished these wanderings. In the midst of my hatred and terror (it means nothing to me now to speak of terror, now that I have foiled Richard Madden, now that my throat yearns for the noose) it occurred to me that that tumultuous and doubtless happy warrior did not suspect that I possessed the Secret. The name of the exact location of the new British artillery park on the River Ancre. A bird streaked across the grey sky and blindly I translated it into an aeroplane and that aeroplane into many (against the French sky) annihilating the artillery station with vertical bombs. If only my mouth, before a bullet shattered it, could cry out that secret name so it could be heard in Germany . . . My human voice was very weak. How might I make it carry to the ear of the Chief? To the ear of that sick and hateful man who knew nothing of Runeberg and me save that we were in Staffordshire and who was waiting in vain for our report in his arid office in Berlin, endlessly examining newspapers . . . I said out loud: *I must flee.* I sat up noiselessly, in a useless perfection of silence, as if Madden were already lying in wait for me. Something – perhaps the mere vain ostentation of proving my resources were nil – made me look through my pockets. I found what I knew I would find. The American watch, the nickel chain and the square coin, the key ring with the incrimi-

nating useless keys to Runeberg's apartment, the
notebook, a letter which I resolved to destroy immediately (and which I did not destroy), a crown, two shillings
and a few pence, the red and blue pencil, the handker-
chief, the revolver with one bullet. Absurdly, I took it in
my hand and weighed it in order to inspire courage
within myself. Vaguely I thought that a pistol report can
be heard at a great distance. In ten minutes my plan was
perfected. The telephone book listed the name of the
only person capable of transmitting the message; he
lived in a suburb of Fenton, less than a half hour's train
ride away.

I am a cowardly man. I say it now, now that I have
carried to its end a plan whose perilous nature no one
can deny. I know its execution was terrible. I didn't do it
for Germany, no. I care nothing for a barbarous country
which imposed upon me the abjection of being a spy.
Besides, I know of a man from England – a modest
man – who for me is no less great than Goethe. I talked
with him for scarcely an hour, but during that hour he
was Goethe . . . I did it because I sensed that the Chief
somehow scorned people of my race – for the innumerable ancestors who merge within me. I wanted to prove
to him that a yellow man could save his armies. Besides,
I had to flee from Captain Madden. His hands and his
voice could call at my door at any moment. I dressed

silently, bade farewell to myself in the mirror, went downstairs, scrutinized the peaceful street and went out. The station was not far from my home, but I judged it wise to take a cab. I argued that in this way I ran less risk of being recognized; the fact is that in the deserted street I felt myself visible and vulnerable, infinitely so. I remember that I told the cab driver to stop a short distance before the main entrance. I got out with voluntary, almost painful slowness; I was going to the village of Ashgrove but I bought a ticket for a more distant station. The train left within a very few minutes, at eight-fifty. I hurried; the next one would leave at nine-thirty. There was hardly a soul on the platform. I went through the coaches; I remember a few farmers, a woman dressed in mourning, a young boy who was reading with fervour the *Annals* of Tacitus, a wounded and happy soldier. The coaches jerked forward at last. A man whom I recognized ran in vain to the end of the platform. It was Captain Richard Madden. Shattered, trembling, I shrank into the far corner of the seat, away from the dreaded window.

From this broken state I passed into an almost abject happiness. I told myself that the duel had already begun and that I had won the first encounter by frustrating, even if for forty minutes, even if by a stroke of fate, the attack of my adversary. I argued that the victory was not slight, since without the precious difference that the train schedule afforded me, I would be in jail or dead. I argued (no less fallaciously) that my cowardly happiness proved that I was a man capable of carrying out the adventure successfully. From this weakness I took strength that did not abandon me. I foresee that man will resign himself each day to more atrocious undertakings; soon there will be no one but warriors and brigands; I give them this counsel: *The author of an atrocious undertaking ought to imagine that he has already accomplished it, ought to impose upon himself a future as irrevocable as the past.* Thus I proceeded as my eyes of a man already dead registered the elapsing of that day, which was perhaps the last, and the diffusion of the night. The train ran gently along, amid ash trees. It stopped, almost in the middle of the fields. No one announced the name of the station. 'Ashgrove?' I asked a few lads on the platform. 'Ashgrove,' they replied. I got off.

A lamp enlightened the platform but the faces of the boys were in shadow. One questioned me, 'Are you going to Dr Stephen Albert's house?' Without waiting for my answer, another said, 'The house is a long way from here, but you won't get lost if you take this road to the left and at every crossroads turn again to your left.' I tossed them a coin (my last), descended a few stone steps and started down the solitary road. It went downhill, slowly. It was of elemental earth; overhead the branches were tangled; the low full moon seemed to accompany me.

For an instant, I thought that Richard Madden in some way had penetrated my desperate plan. Very quickly, I understood that that was impossible. The instructions to turn always to the left reminded me that such was the common procedure for discovering the central point of certain labyrinths. I have some understanding of labyrinths: not for nothing am I the great grandson of that Ts'ui Pên who was governor of Yunnan and who renounced worldly power in order to write a novel that might be even more populous than the *Hung Lu Meng* and to construct a labyrinth in which all men would become lost. Thirteen years he dedicated to these heterogeneous tasks, but the hand of a stranger murdered him – and his novel was incoherent and no one found the labyrinth. Beneath English trees I meditated on that lost maze: I imagined it inviolate and perfect at the secret crest of a mountain; I imagined it erased by rice fields or beneath the water; I imagined it infinite, no longer composed of octagonal kiosks and returning paths, but of rivers and provinces and kingdoms . . . I thought of a labyrinth of labyrinths, of one sinuous spreading labyrinth that would encompass the past and the future and in some way involve the stars. Absorbed in these illusory images, I forgot my destiny of one pursued. I felt myself to be, for an unknown period of time, an abstract perceiver of the world. The vague, living countryside, the moon, the remains of the day worked on me, as well as the slope of the road which eliminated any possibility of weariness. The evening was intimate, infinite. The road descended and forked among the now confused meadows. A high-pitched, almost syllabic music approached and receded in the shifting of the wind, dimmed by leaves and distance. I thought that a man can be an enemy of other men, of the moments of other men, but not of a country: not of fireflies, words, gardens, streams of water, sunsets. Thus I arrived before a tall, rusty gate. Between the iron bars I made out a poplar grove and a pavilion. I understood suddenly two things, the first trivial, the second almost unbelievable: the music came from the pavilion, and the music was Chinese. For precisely that reason I had openly accepted it without paying it any heed. I do not recall if there was a bell or a buzzer or if I clapped my hands. The sparkling of the music continued.

From the rear of the secluded house within a lantern approached: a lantern that the trees sometimes striped and sometimes eclipsed, a paper lantern that had the form of a drum and the colour of the moon. A tall man bore it. I didn't see his face for the light blinded me. He opened the door and said slowly, in my own language: 'I see that the pious Hsi P'êng persists in correcting my solitude. You no doubt wish to see the garden?'

I recognized the name of one of our consuls and I replied, disconcerted, 'The garden?'

'The garden of forking paths.'

Something stirred in my memory and I uttered with incomprehensible certainty, 'The garden of my ancestor Ts'ui Pên.'

'Your ancestor? Your illustrious ancestor? Come in.'

The damp path zigzagged like those of my childhood. We came to a library of Eastern and Western books. I recognized bound in yellow silk several volumes of the Lost Encyclopaedia, edited by the Third Emperor of the Luminous Dynasty but never printed. The record on the phonograph revolved next to a bronze phoenix. I also recall a *famille rose* vase and another, many centuries older, of that shade of blue which our craftsmen copied from the potters of Persia . . .

Stephen Albert observed me with a smile. He was, as I have said, very tall, sharp-featured, with grey eyes and a grey beard. There was something of a priest about him and also of a sailor; later he told me that he had been a missionary in Tientsin 'before aspiring to become a Sinologist'.

We sat down – I on a long, low divan, he with his back to the window and a tall circular clock. I calculated that my pursuer, Richard Madden, could not arrive for at least an hour. My irrevocable determination could wait.

'An astounding fate, that of Ts'ui Pên,' Stephen Albert said. 'Governor of his native province, learned in astronomy, in astrology and in the tireless interpretation of the canonical books, chess player, famous poet and calligrapher – he abandoned all this in order to compose a book and a maze. He renounced the pleasures of both tyranny and justice, of his populous couch, of his banquets and even of erudition – all to close himself up for thirteen years in the Pavilion of the Limpid Solitude. When he died, his heirs found nothing save chaotic manuscripts. His family, as you may be aware, wished to condemn them to the fire, but his executor – a Taoist or Buddhist monk – insisted on their publication.'

'We descendants of Ts'ui Pên,' I replied, 'continue to curse that monk. Their publication was senseless. The book is an indeterminate heap of contradictory drafts. I examined it once: in the third chapter the hero dies, in the fourth he is alive. As for the other undertaking of Ts'ui Pên, his labyrinth . . .'

'Here is Ts'ui Pên's labyrinth,' he said, indicating a tall lacquered desk.

'An ivory labyrinth!' I exclaimed. 'A tiny labyrinth.'

'A labyrinth of symbols,' he corrected. 'An invisible labyrinth of time. To me, a barbarous Englishman, has been entrusted the revelation of this diaphanous mystery. After more than a hundred years, the details are irretrievable; but it is not hard to conjecture what happened. Ts'ui Pên must have said once: *I am withdrawing to write a book.* And another time: *I am withdrawing to construct a labyrinth.* Every one imagined two works; to no one did it occur that the book and the maze were one and the same thing. The Pavilion of the Limpid Solitude stood in the centre of a garden that was perhaps intricate; that circumstance may have suggested to men a physical labyrinth. Ts'ui Pên died; no one in the vast territories that were his came upon the labyrinth; the confusion of the novel suggested to me that *it* was the maze. Two circumstances gave me the correct solution of the problem. One: the curious legend that Ts'ui Pên had planned to create a labyrinth which would be strictly infinite. The other: a fragment of a letter I discovered.'

Albert rose. He turned his back on me for a moment; he opened a drawer of the black and gold desk. He faced me and in his hands he held a sheet of paper that had once been crimson, but was now pink and tenuous and cross-sectioned. The fame of Ts'ui Pên as a calligrapher had been justly won. I read, uncomprehendingly and with fervour, these words written with a minute brush by a man of my blood: *I leave to the various futures (not to all) my garden of forking paths.* Wordlessly, I returned the sheet. Albert continued:

'Before unearthing this letter, I had questioned myself

about the ways in which a book can be infinite. I could think of nothing other than a cyclical volume, a circular one. A book whose last page was identical with the first, a book which had the possibility of continuing indefinitely. I remembered too that night which is at the middle of the Thousand and One Nights when Queen Scheherazade (through a magical oversight of the copyist) begins to relate word for word the story of the Thousand and One Nights, at the risk of coming once again to the night when she must repeat it, and thus on to infinity. I imagined as well a Platonic, hereditary work, transmitted from father to son, in which each new individual added a chapter or corrected with pious care the pages of his elders. These conjectures diverted me; but none seemed to correspond, not even remotely, to the contradictory chapters of Ts'ui Pên. In the midst of this perplexity, I received from Oxford the manuscript you have examined. I lingered, naturally, on the sentence: *I leave to the various futures (not to all) my garden of forking paths.* Almost instantly, I understood: "the garden of forking paths" was the chaotic novel; the phrase "the various futures (not to all)" suggested to me the forking in time, not in space. A broad rereading of the work confirmed the theory. In all fictional works, each time a man is confronted with several alternatives, he chooses one and eliminates the others; in the fiction of the almost inextricable Ts'ui Pên, he chooses – simultaneously – all of them. *He creates*, in this way, diverse futures, diverse times which themselves also proliferate and fork. Here, then, is the explanation of the novel's contradictions. Fang, let us say, has a secret; a stranger calls at his door; Fang resolves to kill him. Naturally, there are several outcomes: Fang can kill the intruder, the intruder can kill Fang, they both can escape, they both can die, and so forth. In the work of Ts'ui Pên, all possible outcomes occur; each one is the point of departure for other forkings. Sometimes, the paths of this labyrinth converge: for example, you arrive at this house, but in one of the possible pasts you are my enemy, in another, my friend. If you will resign yourself to my incurable pronunciation, we shall read a few pages.'

His face, within the vivid circle of the lamplight, was unquestionably that of an old man, but with something unalterable about it, even immortal. He read with slow precision two versions of the same epic chapter. In the first, an army marches to a battle across a desolate mountain; the horror of the rocks and shadows makes the men undervalue their lives and they gain an easy victory. In the second, the same army traverses a palace where a great festival is taking place; the resplendent battle seems to them a continuation of the celebration and they win the victory. I listened with proper veneration to these ancient narratives, perhaps less admirable in themselves than the fact that they had been created by my blood and were being restored to me by a man of remote empire, in the course of a desperate adventure, on a Western isle. I remember the last words, repeated in each version like a secret commandment: *Thus fought the heroes, tranquil their admirable hearts, violent their swords, resigned to kill and to die.*

From that moment on, I felt about me and within my dark body an invisible, intangible swarming. Not the swarming of the divergent, parallel and finally coalescent armies, but a more inaccessible, more intimate agitation that they in some manner prefigured. Stephen Albert continued:

'I don't believe that your illustrious ancestor played idly with these variations. I don't consider it credible that he would sacrifice thirteen years to the infinite execution of a rhetorical experiment. In your country, the novel is a subsidiary form of literature; in Ts'ui Pên's time it was a despicable form. Ts'ui Pên was a brilliant novelist, but he was also a man of letters who doubtless did not consider himself a mere novelist. The testimony of his contemporaries proclaims – and his life fully confirms – his metaphysical and mystical interests. Philosophic controversy usurps a good part of the novel. I know that of all problems, none disturbed him so greatly nor worked upon him so much as the abysmal problem of time. Now then, the latter is the only problem that does not figure in the pages of the *Garden*. He does not even use the word that signifies *time*. How do you explain this voluntary omission?'

I proposed several solutions – all inadequate. We discussed them. Finally, Stephen Albert said to me:

'In a riddle whose answer is chess, what is the only prohibited word?'

I thought a moment and replied, 'The word *chess*.'

'Precisely,' said Albert. '*The Garden of Forking Paths* is an enormous riddle, or parable, whose theme is time; this recondite cause prohibits its mention. To omit a word *always*, to resort to inept metaphors and obvious periphrases, is perhaps the most emphatic way of stressing it. That is the tortuous method preferred, in each of the meanderings of his indefatigable novel, by the oblique Ts'ui Pên. I have compared hundreds of manuscripts, I have corrected the errors that the negligence of the copyists has introduced, I have guessed the plan of this chaos, I have re-established – I believe I have re-established – the primordial organization, I have translated the entire work: it is clear to me that not once does he employ the word "time". The explanation is obvious: *The Garden of Forking Paths* is an incomplete, but not false, image of the universe as Ts'ui Pên conceived it. In contrast to Newton and Schopenhauer, your ancestor did not believe in a uniform, absolute time. He believed in an infinite series of times, in a growing, dizzying net of divergent, convergent and parallel times. This network of times which approached one another, forked, broke off, or were unaware of one another for centuries, embraces *all* possibilities of time. We do not exist in the majority of these times; in some you exist, and not I; in others I, and not you; in others, both of us. In the present one, which a favourable fate has granted me, you have arrived at my house; in another, while crossing the garden, you found me dead; in still another, I utter these same words, but I am a mistake, a ghost.'

'In every one,' I pronounced, not without a tremble to my voice, 'I am grateful to you and revere you for your re-creation of the garden of Ts'ui Pên.'

'Not in all,' he murmured with a smile. 'Time forks perpetually towards innumerable futures. In one of them I am your enemy.'

Once again I felt the swarming sensation of which I have spoken. It seemed to me that the humid garden that surrounded the house was infinitely saturated with invisible persons. Those persons were Albert and I, secret, busy and multiform in other dimensions of time. I raised my eyes and the tenuous nightmare dissolved. In the yellow and black garden there was only one man; but this man was as strong as a statue . . . this man was approaching along the path and he was Captain Richard Madden.

'The future already exists,' I replied, 'but I am your friend. Could I see the letter again?'

Albert rose. Standing tall, he opened the drawer of the tall desk; for a moment he turned his back to me. I had readied the revolver. I fired with extreme caution. Albert fell uncomplainingly, immediately. I swear his death was instantaneous – a lightning stroke.

The rest is unreal, insignificant. Madden broke in, arrested me. I have been condemned to the gallows. I have won out abominably; I have communicated to Berlin the secret name of the city they must attack. They bombed it yesterday; I read it in the same papers that offered to England the mystery of the learned Sinologist Stephen Albert who was murdered by a stranger, Yu Tsun. The Chief had deciphered this mystery. He knew my problem was to indicate (through the uproar of the war) the city called Albert, and that I had found no other means to do so than to kill a man of that name. He does not know (no one can know) my innumerable contrition and weariness.

For Victoria Ocampo

The Book of Sand

. . . thy rope of sands . . .
George Herbert (1593–1623)

The line consists of an infinite number of points; the plane, of an infinite number of lines; the volume, of an infinite number of planes; the hypervolume, of an infinite number of volumes . . . No – this, *more geometrico*, is decidedly not the best way to begin my tale. To say that the story is true is by now a convention of every fantastic tale; mine, nevertheless, *is* true.

I live alone, in a fifth-floor apartment on Calle Belgrano. One evening a few months ago, I heard a knock at my door. I opened it, and a stranger stepped in. He was a tall man, with blurred, vague features, or perhaps my nearsightedness made me see him that way. Everything about him spoke of honest poverty: he was dressed in gray, and carried a gray valise. I immediately sensed that he was a foreigner. At first I thought he was old; then I noticed that I had been misled by his sparse hair, which was blond, almost white, like the Scandinavians'. In the course of our conversation, which I doubt lasted more than an hour, I learned that he hailed from the Orkneys.

I pointed the man to a chair. He took some time to begin talking. He gave off an air of melancholy, as I myself do now.

'I sell Bibles,' he said at last.

'In this house,' I replied, not without a somewhat stiff, pedantic note, 'there are several English Bibles, including the first one, Wyclif's. I also have Cipriano de Valera's, Luther's (which is, in literary terms, the worst of the lot), and a Latin copy of the Vulgate. As you see, it isn't exactly Bibles I might be needing.'

After a brief silence he replied.

'It's not only Bibles I sell. I can show you a sacred book that might interest a man such as yourself. I came by it in northern India, in Bikaner.'

He opened his valise and brought out the book. He laid it on the table. It was a clothbound octavo volume that had clearly passed through many hands. I examined it; the unusual heft of it surprised me. On the spine was printed *Holy Writ,* and then *Bombay.*

'Nineteenth century, I'd say,' I observed.

'I don't know,' was the reply. 'Never did know.'

I opened it at random. The characters were unfamiliar

to me. The pages, which seemed worn and badly set, were printed in double columns, like a Bible. The text was cramped, and composed into versicles. At the upper corner of each page were Arabic numerals. I was struck by an odd fact: the even-numbered page would carry the number 40,514, let us say, while the odd-numbered page that followed it would be 999. I turned the page; the next page bore an eight-digit number. It also bore a small illustration, like those one sees in dictionaries: an anchor drawn in pen and ink, as though by the unskilled hand of a child.

It was at that point that the stranger spoke again.

'Look at it well. You will never see it again.'

There was a threat in the words, but not in the voice.

I took note of the page, and then closed the book. Immediately I opened it again. In vain I searched for the figure of the anchor, page after page. To hide my discomfiture, I tried another tack.

'This is a version of Scripture in some Hindu language, isn't that right?'

'No,' he replied.

Then he lowered his voice, as though entrusting me with a secret.

'I came across this book in a village on the plain, and I traded a few rupees and a Bible for it. The man who owned it didn't know how to read. I suspect he saw the

Book of Books as an amulet. He was of the lowest caste; people could not so much as step on his shadow without being defiled. He told me his book was called the Book of Sand because neither sand nor this book has a beginning or an end.'

He suggested I try to find the first page.

I took the cover in my left hand and opened the book, my thumb and forefinger almost touching. It was impossible: several pages always lay between the cover and my hand. It was as though they grew from the very book.

'Now try to find the end.'

I failed there as well.

'This can't be,' I stammered, my voice hardly recognizable as my own.

'It can't be, yet it *is*,' The Bible peddler said, his voice little more than a whisper. 'The number of pages in this book is literally infinite. No page is the first page; no page is the last. I don't know why they're numbered in this arbitrary way, but perhaps it's to give one to understand that the terms of an infinite series can be numbered any way whatever.'

Then, as though thinking out loud, he went on.

'If space is infinite, we are anywhere, at any point in space. If time is infinite, we are at any point in time.'

His musings irritated me.

'You,' I said, 'are a religious man, are you not?'

'Yes, I'm Presbyterian. My conscience is clear. I am certain I didn't cheat that native when I gave him the Lord's Word in exchange for his diabolic book.'

I assured him he had nothing to reproach himself for, and asked whether he was just passing through the country. He replied that he planned to return to his own country within a few days. It was then that I learned he was a Scot, and that his home was in the Orkneys. I told him I had great personal fondness for Scotland because of my love for Stevenson and Hume.

'And Robbie Burns,' he corrected.

As we talked I continued to explore the infinite book.

'Had you intended to offer this curious specimen to the British Museum, then?' I asked with feigned indifference.

'No,' he replied, 'I am offering it to you,' and he mentioned a great sum of money.

I told him, with perfect honesty, that such an amount of money was not within my ability to pay. But my mind was working; in a few moments I had devised my plan.

'I propose a trade,' I said. 'You purchased the volume with a few rupees and the Holy Scripture; I will offer you the full sum of my pension, which I have just received, and Wyclif's black-letter Bible. It was left to me by my parents.'

'A black-letter Wyclif!' he murmured.

I went to my bedroom and brought back the money and the book. With a bibliophile's zeal he turned the pages and studied the binding.

'Done,' he said.

I was astonished that he did not haggle. Only later was I to realize that he had entered my house already determined to sell the book. He did not count the money, but merely put the bills into his pocket.

We chatted about India, the Orkneys, and the Norwegian jarls that had once ruled those islands. Night was falling when the man left. I have never seen him since, nor do I know his name.

I thought of putting the Book of Sand in the space left by the Wyclif, but I chose at last to hide it behind some imperfect volumes of the *Thousand and One Nights*.

I went to bed but could not sleep. At three or four in the morning I turned on the light. I took out the impossible book and turned its pages. On one, I saw an engraving of a mask. There was a number in the corner of the page – I don't remember now what it was – raised to the ninth power.

I showed no one my treasure. To the joy of possession was added the fear that it would be stolen from me, and to that, the suspicion that it might not be truly infinite. Those two points of anxiety aggravated my already habitual misanthropy. I had but few friends left, and those, I stopped seeing. A prisoner of the Book, I hardly left my house. I examined the worn binding and the covers with a magnifying glass, and rejected the possibility of some artifice. I found that the small illustrations were spaced at two-thousand-page intervals. I began noting them down in an alphabetized notebook, which was very soon filled. They never repeated themselves. At night, during the rare intervals spared me by insomnia, I dreamed of the book.

Summer was drawing to a close, and I realized that the book was monstrous. It was cold consolation to think that I, who looked upon it with my eyes and fondled it with my ten flesh-and-bone fingers, was no less monstrous than the book. I felt it was a nightmare thing, an obscene thing, and that it defiled and corrupted reality.

I considered fire, but I feared that the burning of an infinite book might be similarly infinite, and suffocate the planet in smoke.

I remembered reading once that the best place to hide a leaf is in the forest. Before my retirement I had worked in the National Library, which contained nine hundred thousand books; I knew that to the right of the lobby a curving staircase descended into the shadows of the basement, where the maps and periodicals are kept.

I took advantage of the librarians' distraction to hide the Book of Sand on one of the library's damp shelves; I tried not to notice how high up, or how far from the door.

I now feel a little better, but I refuse even to walk down the street the library's on.

The Circular Ruins

And if he left off dreaming about you . . .

Through the Looking Glass, VI

No one saw him disembark in the unanimous night, no one saw the bamboo canoe sinking into the sacred mud, but within a few days no one was unaware that the silent man came from the South and that his home was one of the infinite villages upstream, on the violent mountainside, where the Zend tongue is not contaminated with Greek and where leprosy is infrequent. The truth is that the obscure man kissed the mud, came up the bank without pushing aside (probably without feeling) the brambles which dilacerated his flesh, and dragged himself, nauseous and bloodstained, to the circular enclosure crowned by a stone tiger or horse, which once was the colour of fire and now was that of ashes. This circle was a temple, long ago devoured by fire, which the malarial jungle had profaned and whose god no longer received the homage of men. The stranger stretched out beneath the pedestal. He was awakened by the sun high above. He evidenced without astonishment that his wounds had closed; he shut his pale eyes and slept, not out of bodily weakness but out of determination of will. He knew that this temple was the place required by his invincible purpose; he knew that, downstream, the incessant trees had not managed to choke the ruins of another propitious temple, whose gods were also burned and dead; he knew that his immediate obligation was to sleep. Towards midnight he was awakened by the disconsolate cry of a bird. Prints of bare feet, some figs and a jug told him that men of the region had respectfully spied upon his sleep and were solicitous of his favour or feared his magic. He felt the chill of fear and sought out a burial niche in the dilapidated wall and covered himself with some unknown leaves.

The purpose which guided him was not impossible, though it was supernatural. He wanted to dream a man: he wanted to dream him with minute integrity and insert him into reality. This magical project had exhausted the entire content of his soul; if someone had asked him his own name or any trait of his previous life, he would not have been able to answer. The uninhabited and broken temple suited him, for it was a minimum of visible world; the nearness of the peasants also suited him, for they would see that his frugal necessities were supplied. The rice and fruit of their tribute were suffi-cient sustenance for his body, consecrated to the sole task of sleeping and dreaming.

At first, his dreams were chaotic; somewhat later, they were of a dialectical nature. The stranger dreamt that he was in the centre of a circular amphitheatre which in some way was the burned temple: clouds of silent students filled the gradins; the faces of the last ones hung many centuries away and at a cosmic height, but were entirely clear and precise. The man was lecturing to them on anatomy, cos-mography, magic; the countenances listened with eagerness and strove to respond with understanding, as if they divined the importance of the examination which would redeem one of them from his state of vain appear-ance and interpolate him into the world of reality. The man, both in dreams and awake, considered his phantoms' replies, was not deceived by impostors, divined a growing intelligence in certain perplexities. He sought a soul which would merit participation in the universe.

After nine or ten nights, he comprehended with some bitterness that he could expect nothing of those students who passively accepted his doctrines, but that he could of those who, at times, would venture a reasonable contradiction. The former, though worthy of love and affection, could not rise to the state of individuals; the latter pre-existed somewhat more. One afternoon (now his afternoons too were tributaries of sleep, now he remained awake only for a couple of hours at dawn) he dismissed the vast illusory college for ever and kept one single student. He was a silent boy, sallow, sometimes obstinate, with sharp features which reproduced those of the dreamer. He was not long disconcerted by his companions' sudden elimination; his progress, after a few special lessons, astounded his teacher. Nevertheless, catastrophe ensued. The man emerged from sleep one day as if from a viscous desert, looked at the vain light of afternoon, which at first he confused with that of dawn, and understood that he had not really dreamt. All that night and all day, the intolerable lucidity of insomnia weighed upon him. He tried to explore the jungle, to exhaust himself; amidst the hemlocks, he was scarcely able to manage a few snatches of feeble sleep, fleetingly mottled with some rudimentary visions which were useless. He tried to convoke the college and had scarcely uttered a few brief words of exhortation, when it became deformed and was extinguished. In his almost perpetual sleeplessness, his old eyes burned with tears of anger.

He comprehended that the effort to mould the incoherent and vertiginous matter dreams are made of was the most arduous task a man could undertake, though he might penetrate all enigmas of the upper and lower orders: much more arduous than weaving a rope of sand or coining the faceless wind. He comprehended that an initial failure was inevitable. He swore he would forget the enormous hallucination which had misled him at first, and he sought another method. Before putting it into effect, he dedicated a month to replenishing the powers his delirium had wasted. He abandoned any premeditation of dreaming and, almost at once, was able to sleep for a considerable part of the day. The few times he dreamt during this period, he did not take notice of the dreams. To take up his task again, he waited until the moon's disk was perfect. Then, in the afternoon, he purified himself in the waters of the river, worshipped the planetary gods, uttered the lawful syllables of a powerful name and slept. Almost immediately, he dreamt of a beating heart.

He dreamt it as active, warm, secret, the size of a closed fist, of garnet colour in the penumbra of a human body as yet without face or sex; with minute love he dreamt it, for fourteen lucid nights. Each night he perceived it with greater clarity. He did not touch it, but limited himself to witnessing it, observing it, perhaps correcting it with his eyes. He perceived it, lived it, from many distances and many angles. On the fourteenth night he touched the pulmonary artery with his finger, and then the whole heart, inside and out. The examination satisfied him. Deliberately, he did not dream for a night; then he took the heart again, invoked the name of a planet and set about to envision another of the principal organs. Within a year he reached the skeleton, the eyelids. The innumerable hair was perhaps the most difficult task. He dreamt a complete man, a youth, but this youth could not rise nor did he speak nor could he open his eyes. Night after night, the man dreamt him as asleep.

In the Gnostic cosmogonies, the demiurgi knead and mould a red Adam who cannot stand alone; as unskilful and crude and elementary as this Adam of dust was the Adam of dreams fabricated by the magician's nights of effort. One afternoon, the man almost destroyed his work, but then repented. (It would have been better for him had he destroyed it.) Once he had completed his supplications to the numina of the earth and the river, he threw himself down at the feet of the effigy which was perhaps a tiger and perhaps a horse, and implored its unknown succour. That twilight, he dreamt of the statue. He dreamt of it as a living, tremulous thing: it was not an atrocious mongrel of tiger and horse, but both these vehement creatures at once and also a bull, a rose, a tempest. This multiple god revealed to him that its earthly name was Fire, that in the circular temple (and in others of its kind) people had rendered it sacrifices and cult and that it would magically give life to the sleeping phantom, in such a way that all creatures except Fire itself and the dreamer would believe him to be a man of flesh and blood. The man was ordered by the divinity to instruct his creature in its rites, and send him to the other broken temple whose pyramids survived downstream, so that in this deserted edifice a voice might give glory to the god. In the dreamer's dream, the dreamed one awoke.

The magician carried out these orders. He devoted a period of time (which finally comprised two years) to revealing the arcana of the universe and of the fire cult to his dream child. Inwardly, it pained him to be separated from the boy. Under the pretext of pedagogical necessity, each day he prolonged the hours he dedicated to his dreams. He also redid the right shoulder, which was perhaps deficient. At times, he was troubled by the impression that all this had happened before . . . In general, his days were happy; when he closed his eyes, he would think: *Now I shall be with my son.* Or, less often: *The child I have engendered awaits me and will not exist if I do not go to him.*

Gradually, he accustomed the boy to reality. Once he ordered him to place a banner on a distant peak. The following day, the banner flickered from the mountain top. He tried other analogous experiments, each more daring than the last. He understood with certain bitterness that his son was ready – and perhaps impatient – to be born. That night he kissed him for the first time and sent him to the other temple whose debris showed white downstream, through many leagues of inextricable jungle and swamp. But first (so that he would never know he was a phantom, so that he would be thought a man like others) he instilled into him a complete oblivion of his years of apprenticeship.

The man's victory and peace were dimmed by weariness. At dawn and at twilight, he would prostrate himself before the stone figure, imagining perhaps that his unreal child was practising the same rites, in other circular ruins, downstream; at night, he would not dream, or would dream only as all men do. He perceived the sounds and forms of the universe with a certain colourlessness: his absent son was being nurtured with these diminutions of his soul. His life's purpose was complete; the man persisted in a kind of ecstasy. After a time, which some narrators of his story prefer to compute in years and others in lustra, he was awakened one midnight by two boatmen; he could not see their faces, but they told him of a magic man in a temple of the North who could walk upon fire and not be burned. The magician suddenly remembered the words of the god. He recalled that, of all the creatures of the world, fire was the only one that knew his son was a phantom. This recollection, at first soothing, finally tormented him. He feared his son might meditate on his abnormal privilege and discover in some way that his condition was that of a mere image. Not to be a man, to be the projection of another man's dream, what a feeling of humiliation, of vertigo! All fathers are interested in the children they have procreated (they have permitted to exist) in mere confusion or pleasure; it was natural that the magician should fear for the future of that son, created in thought, limb by limb and feature by feature, in a thousand and one secret nights.

The end of his meditations was sudden, though it was foretold in certain signs. First (after a long drought) a faraway cloud on a hill, light and rapid as a bird; then, towards the south, the sky which had the rose colour of the leopard's mouth; then the smoke which corroded the metallic nights; finally, the panicky flight of the animals. For what was happening had happened many centuries ago. The ruins of the fire god's sanctuary were destroyed by fire. In a birdless dawn the magician saw the concentric blaze close round the walls. For a moment, he thought of taking refuge in the river, but then he knew that death was coming to crown his old age and absolve him of his labours. He walked into the shreds of flame. But they did not bite into his flesh, they caressed him and engulfed him without heat or combustion. With relief, with humiliation, with terror, he understood that he too was a mere appearance, dreamt by another.

On Exactitude in Science

. . . In that Empire, the Art of Cartography attained such Perfection that the map of a single Province occupied the entirety of a City, and the map of the Empire, the entirety of a Province. In time, those Unconscionable Maps no longer satisfied, and the Cartographers Guilds struck a Map of the Empire whose size was that of the Empire, and which coincided point for point with it. The following Generations, who were not so fond of the Study of Cartography as their Forebears had been, saw that that vast Map was Useless, and not without some Pitilessness was it, that they delivered it up to the Inclemencies of Sun and Winters. In the Deserts of the West, still today, there are Tattered Ruins of that Map, inhabited by Animals and Beggars; in all the Land there is no other Relic of the Disciplines of Geography.

Suárez Miranda, *Viajes de varones prudentes*,
Libro IV, Cap. XLV, Lérida, 1658

Death and the Compass

Of the many problems which exercised the reckless discernment of Lönnrot, none was so strange – so rigorously strange, shall we say – as the periodic series of bloody events which culminated at the villa of Triste-le-Roy, amid the ceaseless aroma of the eucalypti. It is true that Erik Lönnrot failed to prevent the last murder, but that he foresaw it is indisputable. Neither did he guess the identity of Yarmolinsky's luckless assassin, but he did succeed in divining the secret morphology behind the fiendish series as well as the participation of Red Scharlach, whose other nickname is Scharlach the Dandy. That criminal (as countless others) had sworn on his honour to kill Lönnrot, but the latter could never be intimidated. Lönnrot believed himself a pure reasoner, an Auguste Dupin, but there was something of the adventurer in him, and even a little of the gambler.

The first murder occurred in the Hôtel du Nord – that tall prism which dominates the estuary whose waters are the colour of the desert. To that tower (which quite glaringly unites the hateful whiteness of a hospital, the numbered divisibility of a jail, and the general appearance of a bordello) there came on the third day of December the delegate from Podolsk to the Third Talmudic Congress, Doctor Marcel Yarmolinsky, a grey-bearded man with grey eyes. We shall never know whether the Hôtel du Nord pleased him; he accepted it with the ancient resignation which had allowed him to endure three years of war in the Carpathians and three thousand years of oppression and pogroms. He was given a room on Floor R, across from the suite which was occupied – not without splendour – by the Tetrarch of Galilee. Yarmolinsky supped, postponed until the following day an inspection of the unknown city, arranged in a *placard* his many books and few personal possessions, and before midnight extinguished his light. (Thus declared the Tetrarch's chauffeur who slept in the adjoining room.) On the fourth, at 11:03 a.m., the editor of the *Yidische Zaitung* put in a call to him; Doctor Yarmolinsky did not answer. He was found in his room, his face already a little dark, nearly nude beneath a large, anachronistic cape. He was lying not far from the door which opened on the hall; a deep knife wound had split his breast. A few hours later, in the same room amid journalists, photographers and policemen, Inspector Treviranus and Lönnrot were calmly discussing the problem.

'No need to look for a three-legged cat here,' Treviranus was saying as he brandished an imperious cigar. 'We all know that the Tetrarch of Galilee owns the finest sapphires in the world. Someone, intending to steal them, must have broken in here by mistake. Yarmolinsky got up; the robber had to kill him. How does it sound to you?'

'Possible, but not interesting,' Lönnrot answered. 'You'll reply that reality hasn't the least obligation to be interesting. And I'll answer you that reality may avoid that obligation but that hypotheses may not. In the hypothesis that you propose, chance intervenes copiously. Here we have a dead rabbi; I would prefer a purely rabbinical explanation, not the imaginary mischances of an imaginary robber.'

Treviranus replied ill-humouredly:

'I'm not interested in rabbinical explanations. I am interested in capturing the man who stabbed this unknown person.'

'Not so unknown,' corrected Lönnrot. 'Here are his complete works.' He indicated in the wall-cupboard a row of tall books: a *Vindication of the Cabala; An Examination of the Philosophy of Robert Fludd*; a literal translation of the *Sepher Yezirah*; a *Biography of the Baal Shem*; a *History of the Hasidic Sect*; a monograph (in German) on the Tetragrammaton; another, on the divine nomenclature of the Pentateuch. The inspector regarded them with dread, almost with repulsion. Then he began to laugh.

'I'm a poor Christian,' he said. 'Carry off those musty volumes if you want; I don't have any time to waste on Jewish superstitions.'

'Maybe the crime belongs to the history of Jewish superstitions,' murmured Lönnrot.

'Like Christianity,' the editor of the *Yidische Zaitung* ventured to add. He was myopic, an atheist and very shy.

No one answered him. One of the agents had found in the small typewriter a piece of paper on which was written the following unfinished sentence:

The first letter of the Name has been uttered

Lönnrot abstained from smiling. Suddenly become a bibliophile or Hebraist, he ordered a package made of the dead man's books and carried them off to his apartment. Indifferent to the police investigation, he dedicated himself to studying them. One large octavo volume revealed to him the teachings of Israel Baal Shem Tobh, founder of the sect of the Pious; another, the virtues and terrors of the Tetragrammaton, which is the unutterable name of God; another, the thesis that God has a secret name, in which is epitomized (as in the crystal sphere which the Persians ascribe to Alexander of Macedonia) his ninth attribute, eternity – that is to say, the immediate knowledge of all things that will be, which are and which have been in the universe. Tradition numbers ninety-nine names of God; the Hebraists attribute that imperfect number to magical fear of even numbers; the Hasidim reason that that hiatus indicates a hundredth name – the Absolute Name.

From this erudition Lönnrot was distracted, a few days later, by the appearance of the editor of the *Yidische Zaitung*. The latter wanted to talk about the murder; Lönnrot preferred to discuss the diverse names of God; the journalist declared, in three columns, that the investigator, Erik Lönnrot, had dedicated himself to studying the names of God in order to come across the name of the murderer. Lönnrot, accustomed to the simplifications of journalism, did not become indignant. One of those enterprising shopkeepers who have discovered that any given man is resigned to buying any given book published a popular edition of the *History of the Hasidic Sect*.

The second murder occurred on the evening of the third of January, in the most deserted and empty corner of the capital's western suburbs. Towards dawn, one of the gendarmes who patrol those solitudes on horseback saw a man in a poncho, lying prone in the shadow of an old paint shop. The harsh features seemed to be masked in blood; a deep knife wound had split his breast. On the wall, across the yellow and red diamonds, were some words written in chalk. The gendarme spelled them out . . . That afternoon, Treviranus and Lönnrot headed for the remote scene of the crime. To the left and right of the automobile the city disintegrated; the firmament grew and houses were of less importance than a brick kiln or a poplar tree. They arrived at their miserable destination: an alley's end, with rose-coloured walls which somehow seemed to reflect the extravagant sunset. The dead man had already been identified. He was Daniel Simon Azevedo, an individual of some fame in the old northern suburbs, who had risen from wagon driver to political tough, then degenerated to a thief and even an informer. (The singular style of his death seemed appropriate to them: Azevedo was the last representative of a generation of bandits who knew how to manipulate a dagger, but not a revolver.) The words in chalk were the following:

The second letter of the Name has been uttered

The third murder occurred on the night of the third of February. A little before one o'clock, the telephone in Inspector Treviranus's office rang. In avid secretiveness, a man with a guttural voice spoke; he said his name was Ginzberg (or Ginsburg) and that he was prepared to communicate, for reasonable remuneration, the events

41

surrounding the two sacrifices of Azevedo and Yarmolinsky. A discordant sound of whistles and horns drowned
out the informer's voice. Then, the connexion was
broken off. Without yet rejecting the possibility of a
hoax (after all, it was carnival time), Treviranus found
out that he had been called from the Liverpool House,
a tavern on the rue de Toulon, that dingy street where
side by side exist the cosmorama and the coffee shop, the
bawdy house and the bible sellers. Treviranus spoke with
the owner. The latter (Black Finnegan, an old Irish criminal who was immersed in, almost overcome by,
respectability) told him that the last person to use the
phone was a lodger, a certain Gryphius, who had just left
with some friends. Treviranus went immediately to Liverpool House. The owner related the following. Eight
days ago Gryphius had rented a room above the tavern.
He was a sharp-featured man with a nebulous grey
beard, and was shabbily dressed in black; Finnegan (who
used the room for a purpose which Treviranus guessed)
demanded a rent which was undoubtedly excessive;
Gryphius paid the stipulated sum without hesitation. He
almost never went out; he dined and lunched in his
room; his face was scarcely known in the bar. On the
night in question, he came downstairs to make a phone
call from Finnegan's office. A closed cab stopped in front
of the tavern. The driver didn't move from his seat;

several patrons recalled that he was wearing a bear's mask. Two harlequins got out of the cab; they were of short stature and no one failed to observe that they were very drunk. With a tooting of horns, they burst into Finnegan's office; they embraced Gryphius, who appeared to recognize them but responded coldly; they exchanged a few words in Yiddish – he in a low, guttural voice, they in high-pitched, false voices – and then went up to the room. Within a quarter hour the three descended, very happy. Gryphius, staggering, seemed as drunk as the others. He walked – tall and dizzy – in the middle, between the masked harlequins. (One of the women at the bar remembered the yellow, red and green diamonds.) Twice he stumbled; twice he was caught and held by the harlequins. Moving off towards the inner harbour which enclosed a rectangular body of water, the three got into the cab and disappeared. From the foot-board of the cab, the last of the harlequins scrawled an obscene figure and a sentence on one of the slates of the pier shed.

Treviranus saw the sentence. It was virtually predict-able. It said:

The last of the letters of the Name has been uttered

Afterwards, he examined the small room of Gryphius-Ginzberg. On the floor there was a brusque star of blood, in the corners, traces of cigarettes of a Hungarian brand; in a cabinet, a book in Latin – the *Philologus Hebraeo-Graecus* (1739) of Leusden – with several manuscript notes. Treviranus looked it over with indignation and had Lönnrot located. The latter, without removing his hat, began to read while the inspector was interrogating the contradictory witnesses to the possible kidnapping. At four o'clock they left. Out on the twisted rue de Toulon, as they were treading on the dead serpentines of the dawn, Treviranus said:

'And what if all this business tonight were just a mock rehearsal?'

Erik Lönnrot smiled and, with all gravity, read a passage (which was underlined) from the thirty-third dissertation of the *Philologus: Dies Judaeorum incpit a solis occasu usque ad solis occasum diei sequentis.*

'This means,' he added, ' "The Hebrew day begins at sundown and lasts until the following sundown." '

The inspector attempted an irony.

'Is that fact the most valuable one you've come across tonight?'

'No. Even more valuable was a word that Ginzberg used.'

The afternoon papers did not overlook the periodic disappearances. *La Cruz de la Espada* contrasted them with the admirable discipline and order of the last

Hermitical Congress; Ernst Palast, in *El Mártir*, criticized 'the intolerable delays in this clandestine and frugal pogrom, which has taken three months to murder three Jews'; the *Yidische Zaitung* rejected the horrible hypothesis of an anti-Semitic plot, 'even though many penetrating intellects admit no other solution to the triple mystery'; the most illustrious gunman of the south, Dandy Red Scharlach, swore that in his district similar crimes could never occur, and he accused Inspector Franz Treviranus of culpable negligence.

On the night of March first, the inspector received an impressive-looking sealed envelope. He opened it; the envelope contained a letter signed 'Baruch Spinoza' and a detailed plan of the city, obviously torn from a Baedeker. The letter prophesied that on the third of March there would not be a fourth murder, since the paint shop in the west, the tavern on the rue de Toulon and the Hôtel du Nord were 'the perfect vertices of a mystic equilateral triangle'; the map demonstrated in red ink the regularity of the triangle. Treviranus read the *more geometrico* argument with resignation, and sent the letter and the map to Lönnrot – who, unquestionably, was deserving of such madnesses.

Erik Lönnrot studied them. The three locations were in fact equidistant. Symmetry in time (the third of December, the third of January, the third of February);

symmetry in space as well . . . Suddenly, he felt as if he were on the point of solving the mystery. A set of calipers and a compass completed his quick intuition. He smiled, pronounced the word Tetragrammaton (of recent acquisition) and phoned the inspector. He said:

'Thank you for the equilateral triangle you sent me last night. It has enabled me to solve the problem. This Friday the criminals will be in jail, we may rest assured.'

'Then they're not planning a fourth murder?'

'Precisely because they *are* planning a fourth murder we can rest assured.'

Lönnrot hung up. One hour later he was travelling on one of the Southern Railway's trains, in the direction of the abandoned villa of Triste-le-Roy. To the south of the city of our story flows a blind little river of muddy water, defamed by refuse and garbage. On the far side is an industrial suburb where, under the protection of a political boss from Barcelona, gunmen thrive. Lönnrot smiled at the thought that the most celebrated gunman of all – Red Scharlach – would have given a great deal to know of his clandestine visit. Azevedo had been an associate of Scharlach; Lönnrot considered the remote possibility that the fourth victim might be Scharlach himself. Then he rejected the idea . . . He had very nearly deciphered the problem; mere circumstances, reality (names, prison records, faces, judicial and penal proceedings) hardly interested him now. He wanted to travel a bit, he wanted to rest from three months of sedentary investigation. He reflected that the explanation of the murders was in an anonymous triangle and a dusty Greek word. The mystery appeared almost crystalline to him now; he was mortified to have dedicated a hundred days to it.

The train stopped at a silent loading station. Lönnrot got off. It was one of those deserted afternoons that seem like dawns. The air of the turbid, puddled plain was damp and cold. Lönnrot began walking across the countryside. He saw dogs, he saw a car on a siding, he saw the horizon, he saw a silver-coloured horse drinking the crapulous water of a puddle. It was growing dark when he saw the rectangular belvedere of the villa of Triste-le-Roy, almost as tall as the black eucalypti which surrounded it. He thought that scarcely one dawning and one nightfall (an ancient splendour in the east and another in the west) separated him from the moment long desired by the seekers of the Name.

A rusty wrought-iron fence defined the irregular perimeter of the villa. The main gate was closed. Lönnrot, without much hope of getting in, circled the area. Once again before the insurmountable gate, he placed his hand between the bars almost mechanically and encountered the bolt. The creaking of the iron surprised him. With a laborious passivity the whole gate swung back.

Lönnrot advanced among the eucalypti treading on confused generations of rigid, broken leaves. Viewed from anear, the house of the villa of Triste-le-Roy abounded in pointless symmetries and in maniacal repetitions: to one Diana in a murky niche corresponded a second Diana in another niche; one balcony was reflected in another balcony; double stairways led to double balustrades. A two-faced Hermes projected a monstrous shadow. Lönnrot circled the house as he had the villa. He examined everything; beneath the level of the terrace he saw a narrow Venetian blind.

He pushed it; a few marble steps descended to a vault. Lönnrot, who had now perceived the architect's preferences, guessed that at the opposite wall there would be another stairway. He found it, ascended, raised his hands and opened the trap door.

A brilliant light led him to a window. He opened it: a yellow, rounded moon defined two silent fountains in the melancholy garden. Lönnrot explored the house. Through anterooms and galleries he passed to duplicate patios, and time after time to the same patio. He ascended the dusty stairs to circular antechambers; he was multiplied infinitely in opposing mirrors; he grew tired of opening or half-opening windows which revealed outside the same desolate garden from various heights and various angles; inside, only pieces of furniture wrapped in yellow dust sheets and chandeliers bound up in tarlatan. A bedroom detained him; in that bedroom, one single flower in a porcelain vase; at the first touch the ancient petals fell apart. On the second floor, on the top floor, the house seemed infinite and expanding. *The house is not this large,* he thought. *Other things are making it seem larger: the dim light, the symmetry, the mirrors, so many years, my unfamiliarity, the loneliness.*

By way of a spiral staircase he arrived at the oriel. The early evening moon shone through the diamonds of the window; they were yellow, red and green. An astonishing, dizzying recollection struck him.

Two men of short stature, robust and ferocious, threw themselves on him and disarmed him; another, very tall, saluted him gravely and said:

'You are very kind. You have saved us a night and a day.'

It was Red Scharlach. The men handcuffed Lönnrot. The latter at length recovered his voice.

'Scharlach, are you looking for the Secret Name?'

Scharlach remained standing, indifferent. He had not participated in the brief struggle, and he scarcely extended his hand to receive Lönnrot's revolver. He spoke; Lönnrot noted in his voice a fatigued triumph, a hatred the size of the universe, a sadness not less than that hatred.

'No,' said Scharlach. 'I am seeking something more ephemeral and perishable, I am seeking Erik Lönnrot. Three years ago, in a gambling house on the rue de Toulon, you arrested my brother and had him sent to jail. My men slipped me away in a coupé from the gun battle with a policeman's bullet in my stomach. Nine days and nine nights I lay in agony in this desolate, symmetrical villa; fever was demolishing me, and the odious two-faced Janus who watches the twilights and the dawns lent horror to my dreams and to my waking. I came to abominate my body, I came to sense that two eyes, two hands, two lungs are as monstrous as two faces. An Irishman tried to convert me to the faith of Jesus; he repeated to me the phrase of the *goyim*: All roads lead to Rome. At night my delirium nurtured itself on that metaphor; I felt that the world was a labyrinth, from which it was impossible to flee, for all roads, though they pretend to lead to the north or south, actually lead to Rome, which was also the quadrilateral jail where my brother was dying and the villa of Triste-le-Roy. On those nights I swore by the God who sees with two faces and by all the gods of fever and of the mirrors to weave a labyrinth around the man who had imprisoned my brother. I have woven it and it is firm: the ingredients are a dead heresiologist, a compass, an eighteenth-century sect, a Greek word, a dagger, the diamonds of a paint shop.

'The first term of the sequence was given to me by chance. I had planned with a few colleagues – among them Daniel Azevedo – the robbery of the Tetrarch's sapphires. Azevedo betrayed us: he got drunk with the money that we had advanced him and he undertook the job a day early. He got lost in the vastness of the hotel; around two in the morning he stumbled into Yarmolinsky's room. The latter, harassed by insomnia, had started to write. He was working on some notes, apparently, for an article on the Name of God; he had already written the words: *The first letter of the Name has been uttered.* Azevedo warned him to be silent; Yarmolinsky reached out his hand for the bell which would awaken the hotel's forces; Azevedo countered with a single stab in the chest. It was almost a reflex action; half a century of violence had taught him that the easiest and surest thing is to kill . . . Ten days later I learned through the *Yidische Zaitung* that you were seeking in Yarmolinsky's writings the key to his death. I read the *History of the Hasidic Sect*; I learned that the reverent fear of uttering the Name of God had given rise to the doctrine that that Name is all powerful and recondite. I discovered that some Hasidim, in search of that secret Name, had gone so far as to perform human sacrifices . . . I knew that you would make the conjecture that the Hasidim had sacrificed the rabbi; I set myself the task of justifying that conjecture.

'Marcel Yarmolinsky died on the night of December third; for the second "sacrifice" I selected the night of January third. He died in the north; for the second "sacrifice" a place in the west was suitable. Daniel Azevedo was the necessary victim. He deserved death; he was impulsive, a traitor; his apprehension could destroy the entire plan. One of us stabbed him; in order to link his corpse to the other one I wrote on the paint shop diamonds: *The second letter of the Name has been uttered.*

'The third murder was produced on the third of February. It was, as Treviranus guessed, a mere sham. I am Gryphius-Ginzberg-Ginsburg; I endured an interminable week (supplemented by a tenuous fake beard) in the perverse cubicle on the rue de Toulon, until my friends abducted me. From the footboard of the cab, one of them wrote on a post: *The last of the letters of the Name has been uttered.* That sentence revealed that the series of murders was *triple*. Thus the public understood it; I, nevertheless, interspersed repeated signs that would allow you, Erik Lönnrot, the reasoner, to understand that the series was quadruple. A portent in the north, others in the east and west, demand a fourth portent in the south; the Tetragrammaton – the name of God, JHVH – is made up of *four* letters; the harlequins and the paint shop sign suggested *four* points. In the manual of Leusden I underlined a certain passage: that passage manifests that Hebrews compute the day from sunset to sunset; that passage makes known that the deaths occurred on the *fourth* of each month. I sent the equilateral triangle to Treviranus. I foresaw that you would add the missing point. The point which would form a perfect rhomb, the point which fixes in advance where a punctual death awaits you. I have premeditated everything, Erik Lönnrot, in order to attract you to the solitudes of Triste-le-Roy.'

Lönnrot avoided Scharlach's eyes. He looked at the trees and the sky subdivided into diamonds of turbid yellow, green and red. He felt faintly cold, and he felt, too, an impersonal – almost anonymous – sadness. It was already night; from the dusty garden came the futile cry of a bird. For the last time, Lönnrot considered the problem of the symmetrical and periodic deaths.

'In your labyrinth there are three lines too many,' he said at last. 'I know of one Greek labyrinth which is a single straight line. Along that line so many philosophers have lost themselves that a mere detective might well do so, too. Scharlach, when in some other incarnation you hunt me, pretend to commit (or do commit) a crime at A, then a second crime at B, eight kilometres from A, then a third crime at C, four kilometres from A and B, half-way between the two. Wait for me afterwards at D, two kilometres from A and C, again halfway between both. Kill me at D, as you are now going to kill me at Triste-le-Roy.'

'The next time I kill you,' replied Scharlach, 'I promise you that labyrinth, consisting of a single line which is invisible and unceasing.'

He moved back a few steps. Then, very carefully, he fired.

For Mandie Molina Vedia